The Old Woman and the Willy Nilly Man

by jill Wright / Pictures by Glen Rounds

G. P. Putnam's Sons

New York

Library of Congress Cataloging-in-Publication Data
Wright, Jill, date. The old woman and the willy nilly man.
Summary: When the old woman's shoes sing and dance
all night and keep her awake, she goes to the
scary Willy Nilly Man for help.
[1. Shoes—Fiction]   I. Rounds, Glen, ill.
II. Title. PZ7.W949401   1987   [E]   86-9377
ISBN 0-399-21355-4

Once upon a time in the woods, a little old woman lived all by herself. One night she was gittin ready for bed. She brushed her teeth, took off her day clothes, put on her night clothes, and set her little shoes on the floor by the bed.

Then she did something mighty peculiar. She hobbled outside and got two big rocks.

She put one rock on her left shoe and one rock on her right shoe. Then she shook her finger at her shoes and said, "Little shoes, little shoes, stay where I put ye." And she laid down and pulled the quilt up to her chin.

See, the little old woman thought that if she put rocks on her shoes, they wouldn't get up in the night and dance around and sing like they'd been doin for the last ten nights.

But she was wrong! 'Cause soon as she got to snorin, them shoes kicked the rocks off, clatter, clatter, clatter; walked into the other room; talked to each other—"Would you care to dance?" "Don't mind if I do!"—and commenced to carryin on.

"Oh, I knew it wouldn't work!" said the old woman, wakin up out of a sound sleep. She got up and went to the door of her bedroom. "You stop that ruckus! I cain't git no sleep atall with you dancin around like that. Stop it, I said!"

She shook her fist at 'em and tried to catch up to 'em. "I'm gonna git you!" She even chased 'em around with a broom till she was too tired. But the shoes didn't pay her no mind. They just kept dancin and singin till mornin.

"What am I gonna do?" she said to herself the next mornin.
"Gettin no sleep is makin me plumb forgitful."

The little old woman got dressed and went out to pick black-
berries, forgittin she'd done it the day before and the bushes was all
empty. She was so sleepy that after a few minutes in the woods, she
forgot where she was goin. It was then she had a thought: "I'll go see
the Willy Nilly Man and ask him to help me!"

Now the Willy Nilly Man is scairy. He lives in a house in the middle of the woods but it's not like a house regular folks would live in. It's all made up out of pieces of tin and old cans and boxes and junk he's found down along the railroad tracks. And it has a cow skull hangin on it and an old goat skull and a lot of skinny dogs are slinkin around outside growlin.

When the old woman got there, the Willy Nilly Man was sittin in the middle of his clearing beatin on a big old drum, singin, "Clothes, wash yourselves . . . clothes, wash yourselves." And what do you think! His raggedy clothes were rubbin theirselves against the washboard and sudsin up. Then they'd dance on over to the wringer and wring theirselves out and fly across to the clothes line and hang over it. And nobody was helpin 'em.

Now the Willy Nilly Man is scairy. He has one big old eye that looks out one way and another big old eye that rolls around and looks out the other way so's you cain't tell if'n he's lookin at you or not. And he's got a beard down to his knees. And all kind of weird things live in that beard. Spiders live in there and lizards. And sticks and grease and pieces of things he's eaten just hang around on it. And the Willy Nilly Man's one long crooked tooth is black 'cause he never brushed it.

The old woman stood at the edge of the clearing. Her teeth were chattering with fright. Folk said the most terrible things about the Willy Nilly Man. And now, seein him, she could believe they were all true.

She opened her mouth. Then she closed it. She'd forgotten why she'd come. "Now what did I come here fer?" she thought. "Jest to have the daylights scaired outta me? Oh I wish I could remember! Maybe if'n I go back to the house and start again, I'll think of it."

She turned to go, but her foot caught on a clackjack root, and when she'd a-wriggled it loose she had to look at them pesky shoes. "Oh them shoes! That's what I come here fer!" She turned back around to face the clearing and found herself face-to-face with the Willy Nilly Man.

"What you want, old woman?" The Willy Nilly Man's voice was kinda gravelly and deep.

"Y . . . You got to help me, Willy Nilly Man. You jest got to."

"Who are you? What'd I want to help you fer? Go on home." The Willy Nilly Man turned his head but he still seemed to be lookin at her 'cause his eyes're so funny.

"You jest got to help me. My little shoes have got somethin wrong with 'em. They gits up every night and dances and sings all night long. They make such a ruckus that I cain't git no sleep atall."

"What do I care if'n you sleeps or not. Git on outta here now. Don't be botherin me." He looked at the old woman real mean-like. But she'd come too far to leave now.

"Willy Nilly Man, I done heard you could do powerful strange things. You're the onliest person hereabouts who could possibly help me. Just tell my little shoes not to do what they been doin no more."

"I don't help nobody!" growled the Willy Nilly Man. "Now you git on outta here!"

The old woman backed off and started for the woods. Seein the woods gave her an idea.

"I'll give you some blackbury jam if'n you'll help me. I'll give you a whole big jar."

Now the Willy Nilly Man loved blackberry jam. In fact he loved eatin. But mostly he loved sweets because his one tooth was a sweet tooth.

"Blackbury jam?" The Willy Nilly Man thought about it for a moment. Then he said, "Go on home now, and tonight everything'll be dif'rent."

The little old woman tottered home. That night she was very excited. She remembered to brush her teeth, but she laid right down in her day clothes and never even put on her night clothes. It was only when she started to pull the quilt up that she remembered to take off her shoes.

She set 'em down by the side of the bed sayin, "Little shoes, little shoes, stay where I put ye," yawnin so much that she could barely finish. And she didn't put rocks on 'em or nuthin. Then she smiled and stretched out and laid down to the best sleep she'd ever had.

But it didn't last long! Soon as she started snorin—clatter, clatter, clatter. "Would you care to dance?" "Don't mind if I do!" And the carryin on commenced.

The old woman woke up with a start. "Oh no! This cain't be right! The Willy Nilly Man told me that tonight everything's gonna be dif'rent!"

And so it was. For when she crept into the other room and her little shoes saw her, they jumped right onto her feet! And before she knew what was happenin, she commenced to dancin and prancin, whirligigin and jiggin, jumpin and slappin her thighs like she was sixteen years old! And she couldn't stop or git them shoes off for nuthin.

When mornin come, she was pretty near wore out. She was also mad fit to be tied. Never, never in all her ninety-two years had she been so mad. "I's gonna fix that Willy Nilly Man!"

She stirred a pot full of her best blackberry jam. She poured it into a clean jar. And then she went and got her lye soap and put soap into that blackberry jam. Then she got some rocks and put them into the blackberry jam. She swept the ceiling for spiderwebs and put them into the blackberry jam. She put black ink and paste into the blackberry jam. Before she put on the lid, she even put a tooth her old cat had lost into the blackberry jam.

Then she got down her walkin stick and started through the
woods to the Willy Nilly Man's house.

The Willy Nilly Man was sittin outside his house beatin on his drum when she got there. He didn't even look up when she come into the clearing.

"Willy Nilly Man," she called out to him in her nicest voice. "I got somethin fer ye. Blackbury jam." She held it out to him and he stopped drummin and came over. He took the jam and then sat back down on his stump again.

"Why looky here," he said. And he opened up the lid, tipped up the jar, and swallowed it all in one big gulp!

"OOOOHHHHHHHH! MY BELLY HURTS!" He commenced to yellin and rollin around on the ground and the little old woman beat it back to her house as fast as she could.

The Willy Nilly Man rolled around and held his belly for a long time. Then finally it stopped hurting and he sat up. "That old woman," he started to growl to hisself. "That old woman . . . sure fixed me! She surely did!" And somehow when he thought about it, he started to laugh. "I ain't never had nobody fix me like she did." And he laughed and laughed.

Now this was a wonderful thing 'cause the Willy Nilly Man hadn't laughed for fifty years or more. And when he commenced to laughin and thinkin about that old woman, he thought, "Maybe I'll jest go pay her a visit." Now that was strange too 'cause the Willy Nilly Man hadn't paid anybody a visit in more than sixty years.

He pushed his way through the woods over to the old woman's house. The old woman heard him comin. "Where can I hide? Oh, where can I hide?" She bobbed around her little house lookin for hidey holes. She tried under the table and up the chimbley.

"Old woman! Old woman!"

"Oh dear, he's gonna kill me fer sure," said the little old woman as she squeezed under her rickety bed.

"Old woman! Come on out here now, I won't hurt ye!"

The old woman poked her head out from under the bed. Then she peeked out the window. The Willy Nilly Man was smiling!

"Come on out now. Don't be scaired. That funny old blackbury jam you give me made me laugh. Ain't nuthin makes me laugh. I reckoned I'd come over here and thank you. I's thinkin too, seein as how you ain't afraid of me, maybe you'd like to pay me another call sometime. Social like. You don't have to bring no jam," he added hastily.

"I cain't pay nobody no calls if'n I'm dancin around all night ever night."

"Alright, old woman. Your shoes ain't gonna dance no more. Depend on it." And he turned and disappeared into the woods.

That night, the old woman brushed her teeth and took off her day clothes and put on her night clothes and set her little shoes down, talkin to 'em just like always. But once she started snorin, she snored right through the night, cause her little shoes stayed right where she put 'em.